# 100 Wonderful Things
## to Keep Kids Busy and Having Fun

# 100 Wonderful Things
## to Keep Kids Busy and Having Fun

**Pam Schiller and Joan Rossano**

Ten Speed Press
**Berkeley, California**

Ten Speed Press
Box 7123
Berkeley, CA 94707

Text design and type set by Canterbury Press
Cover design by Fifth Street Design

Library of Congress Cataloging-in-Publication Data
    100 wonderful things to keep kids busy and having fun / Pam Schiller & Joan Rossano.
        p.    cm.
    ISBN 0-89815-464-2
    1. Educational games. 2. Creative activities and seat work.  I. Rossano, Joan. II. Title. III. Title: One hundred wonderful things to keep kids busy and having fun.
LB1029.G3S37  1992                          91-38706
372.1'078—dc20                            CIP

First Printing, 1992

Printed in the United States of America

1 2 3 4 5 — 96 95 94 93 92

# Foreword

A note to parents, grandparents, and care givers:

Remember how much fun it was to make paper chains, mud pies, catalog paper dolls, and box wagons? Creating something from nothing filled our childhood days and provided us with such a sense of accomplishment. What did it take to get us started? Simple materials, some ideas, and often someone to direct and guide us along the way. With daddy's help, a newspaper became a sailor's hat. Grandmother's leftover cookie dough was made into snakes, beads, and letters. A cousin's hand-me-down dress was transformed into a coronation gown. What made these experiences special was not just the simplicity of materials but also those special someones who let us enter their world and then applauded our efforts. Isn't it interesting that these "something from nothing experiences" with significant others are among our best memories?

Compare these experiences with those available to children today. In our hurried push-button, overly organized society, it is difficult to create opportunities for informal play and quality interactions. The tendency is to push children into tight molds of conformity and to accept electronic nurturing as the ideal. As children prepare for modern society with all its technological advances, it is important that they take with them the security of knowing how to have fun and enjoy the simple things in life.

There's no need for a gap between the lives of children and the lives of adults and there's no need for the gap between simplicity and complexity. There is a common ground on which to build good times and good memories. *100 Wonderful Things* provides opportunities for establishing that common ground. It is filled with a plethora of ideas to keep children busy and having fun, and guess what? Adults will have fun, too.

This book is for everyone who touches the lives of children. It's easy, it's fun, and the materials are inexpensive. The activities develop children's innate sense of wonder, individuality, and resourcefulness as they prepare to meet the challenges of the next century.

*100 Wonderful Things* offers you 100 of our ideas. You provide the materials and time, and tomorrow's memories begin. Add those ideas from your own memory bank and the memories continue. What a nice oasis from the modern world. We wish you every success in building the continuum of shared memories.

Enjoy the adventure,

Joan and Pam

# Postscripts

1 Activities in this book were created for children between the ages of 3 and 7. However, a number of these activities will still be appealing to older children.

2 Adult and child interaction is a primary feature of this book. As you engage in these activities, consider all issues which relate to the safety of young children, i.e. activities that require heat, tools, special ingredients, and activities that indicate extensions beyond the home environment.

3 All activities in this book are developmentally and educationally sound. Children learn from everything they do. You will notice that on occasion we made a point of identifying the educational benefits underlying the activity.

4 Environmental awareness is a concern for all of us. We have attempted whenever possible to utilize recyclable or reusable materials. This is one small way to help young children to become environmentally conscientious and resourceful.

5 In activities requiring art or construction paper, substitutions may be made. Untreated, plain shelf paper will make a good fingerpaint surface. The backs of letters, computer paper, folders, newspapers, and grocery sacks may also be used for art projects.

# Contents

*tuppaware & lids*

## III.  THINGS TO THINK ABOUT                                27

## IV. THINGS FOR PRETENDING 41

## V. THINGS FOR "MOVING AND GROOVING" 49

## VI. THINGS FOR UNDERSTANDING MY FAMILY AND "ME" 55

# 100 Wonderful Things
## to Keep Kids Busy and Having Fun

ONE

# Things to Make

## Big and Little Circles

**You Will Need:** Tempera paint, paper towels, art paper, crayons, masking tape rings, empty toilet tissue rolls.

### Activity:

► Child creates designs on art paper by tracing the centers of masking tape rings to make big circles.

► Adult pours tempera paint on pads of folded paper towels.

► To make small circles, child presses ends of a cardboard toilet tissue roll on towels with paint and prints small circles on paper.

**HOLIDAY ADAPTATIONS:** Use red and green for Christmas or pink and light green for Easter or spring pictures.

## A Child's Hat

**You Will Need:** Paper plates, a hole punch, ribbon, decorative items (tissue paper strips, gift bows, and so on), glue.

### Activity:

► Cut the centers out of paper plates and punch a hole on each side of the plate for ribbon ties.

► Provide the child with a plate, tissue paper strips, gift bows, and so on.

► Child dots glue on the hat and decorates with the items listed above.

► Place ribbons in the holes to tie under the chin.

**HOLIDAY ADAPTATION:** Make Easter hats and have an Easter Parade.

## Tape Surprise

**You Will Need:** Masking tape, art paper, sponges, tempera paint.

### Activity:

▶ Have the child tear tape and stick it on art paper.

▶ When the tape design is complete, have child sponge over it with paint.

▶ When the paint is nearly dry, child removes the tape to reveal a white design in the paint.

## Torn Paper Art

**You Will Need:** Construction paper; *It Looked Like Spilt Milk*, by Charles Green Shaw (Harper & Row, 1988) (optional); crayons; glue.

### Activity:

▶ Stimulate the child's imagination with a variety of torn paper shapes.

▶ Let the child express what she sees—remembering that there are no wrong answers. *It Looked Like Spilt Milk* is a good book to read to stimulate imagination.

▶ Let child tear paper into her own designs and use crayons for any details needed. She may want to glue the torn paper designs to a background for keeping.

**ADAPTATION:** Extend this activity by looking at the clouds and identifying the shapes.

## Twisted Sculpture

**You Will Need:** Pipe cleaners or coated telephone wire, modeling clay (optional).

### Activity:

► Have child twist pipe cleaners or coated telephone wire into any shape he desires.

► Let child describe his sculpture.

► If desired, place wires in a small amount of modeling clay to make the sculptures freestanding.

## Clay Letters

**You Will Need:** An old cookie sheet, modeling clay, pencils or sticks.

### Activity:

► Fill a cookie sheet with a thin layer of modeling clay.

► Let child use a pencil or stick to draw letters or designs.

► When designs are complete, child may use fingers to press the letters or designs out of the clay.

# Stocking Snakes

**You Will Need:** Panty hose (leg portion only), Styrofoam packaging chips, masking tape or string, marking pens.

## Activity:

► Have child stuff the leg portion cut from panty hose with Styrofoam chips until he has achieved the length desired.

► Fasten the stocking with masking tape or string.

► Child may add eyes, tongue, and stripes with marking pens. The end result is a wiggly snake.

# Stocking Balls

**You Will Need:** Scissors; panty hose; a needle; thread; a bucket, a plastic pool, or masking tape.

## Activity:

► Adult cuts the toe off the left leg of panty hose.

► Begin rolling the stocking from the waist. Gather the right leg into a ball and then roll it into the left leg.

► Turn the cut toe of the left leg back over the rolled-up ball and stitch the ends together.

► When complete, give child a few of these safe balls to throw at a bucket, a plastic pool, or a taped circle.

**Bonus:** Good for large muscle development and coordination.

## Pretzel Letters

**You Will Need:** Ingredients for pretzel dough (see recipe), a pastry brush, egg, coarse salt, an oven.

### Activity:

▶ Adult prepares pretzel dough, as follows:

**Pretzel Dough:**

1 1/2 cups warm water    1 envelope yeast
4 cups flour    1 teaspoon salt

Child can help mix all ingredients.

▶ Give child enough dough to shape into the first letter of his name.

▶ Brush dough letters with beaten egg and sprinkle with coarse salt.

▶ Adult bakes at 425°F for 12 minutes.

## Texture Rubbings

**You Will Need:** Paper; bulletin board letters, leaves, or paper dolls; crayons, items with different textures (sandpapers, net fabric, and so on).

### Activity:

▶ Place a sheet of paper over cardboard bulletin board letters, leaves, or paper dolls.

▶ Child rubs a crayon on the paper until the texture design underneath shows through.

▶ Items with different textures, such as sandpaper or net fabric, also make great rubbings.

## Bean Socks

**You Will Need:** Scissors, old socks, dried beans, a needle, thread, a large container or masking tape.

### Activity:

▶ Adult cuts off old socks at the ankles and partially fills them with dried beans.

▶ Sew up the opening.

▶ Have child toss the beanbags to you or at a target, such as a plastic tub or a circle taped on the floor.

**Bonus:** Great for large muscle development and hand-eye coordination.

## Paper Chains

**You Will Need:** Scissors, construction paper (two or three colors), glue.

### Activity:

▶ Cut sheets of colored paper into 1- by 9-inch strips. Use at least two colors but not more than three colors.

▶ Child glues strips of paper to form a color-patterned chain.

▶ Use chains as necklaces, bracelets, or room decorations.

**HOLIDAY ADAPTATION:** Use red and green at Christmas for house or tree decoration.

## Baggie Book

**You Will Need:** A stapler, six baggies, masking or colored tape, scissors, tagboard or construction paper, crayons or markers, a popular story (such as *Brown Bear, Brown Bear, What Do You See?* by Bill Martin, Jr. [Henry Holt & Co., 1983]).

## Activity:

► Staple baggies together at the bottom of the bags and put a strip of tape over the staples to form the spine of a book.

► Cut pieces of tagboard or construction paper an appropriate size for fitting into the baggies.

► Child dictates and illustrates a story to go on the pages and places the pictures in the proper sequence inside the baggies.

► Change stories by removing current pages and replacing with new ones.

► Use popular stories as models for child to imitate. For example, *Brown Bear, Brown Bear, What Do You See?* may become *Black Cat, Black Cat.* (optional)

**HOLIDAY ADAPTATION:** Let child sequence birthday party photographs.

## Classification Books

**You Will Need:** Construction paper, magazines, newspapers, child's scissors, glue.

### Activity:

▶ Use two pieces of construction paper to make a book.

▶ With the child, look through old magazines and newspapers for pictures of people and animals.

▶ Have child cut out the pictures and paste them on the people page or the animal page.

## Carlos the Caterpillar

**You Will Need:** Writing utensils, green construction paper, masking tape rolls or other round objects to trace, child's scissors, glue.

### Activity:

▶ Have child trace large circles on green paper. (The inside of a roll of masking tape makes an easily traceable shape.)

▶ Number the circles 1, 2, 3, 4, and so on.

▶ Have child cut out circles and glue them together in numerical order, overlapping them slightly.

▶ Provide small strips of paper for "feet."

**Bonus:** Great for recognizing numerals and their appropriate sequence.

## Leaf Rubbings

**You Will Need:** Leaves (a variety of types), light-colored construction paper, crayons.

### Activity:

► To help child notice the veins in leaves and the different shapes of leaves, place a variety of leaves (underside up) under a piece of light-colored construction paper.

► Using the sides of crayons that have had the paper covering removed, child makes crayon rubbings of the leaves.

**Bonus:** Encourages awareness of likenesses and differences!

## Sack Suits

**You Will Need:** Scissors, one paper grocery sack, tempera paint or crayons, a record or musical tape and a player.

### Activity:

► Cut holes in paper grocery sacks for child's head and arms.

► Let child paint or color on the front of the sacks.

► Put on music and let child have a sack suit parade to show off his creations.

**HOLIDAY ADAPTATION:** Stuff uncut sacks with newspaper. Tie top with green yarn. Paint sacks orange to make giant pumpkins. Have a pumpkin patch for Halloween.

# TWO

# Things to Mix, Match, or Move

## Paper Towel Art

**You Will Need:** Food coloring (several colors), water, several jars, several eyedroppers, paper towels or coffee filters, newspaper, a shallow pan.

## Activity:

▶ Using food coloring and water, mix a number of different colors, each in a separate jar. Place an eyedropper in each jar.

▶ Place a paper towel or coffee filter on newspaper padding in a shallow pan.

▶ Child uses eyedroppers to drop color onto paper towels or coffee filters.

▶ As the color spots overlap, child will discover different colors.

**Bonus:** Good for finger muscles.

**19**

## Balls, Ropes, Beads, Bracelets, and Biscuits

**You Will Need:** Playdough ingredients (see recipes), rolling pins, bisquit cutters.

## Activity:

▶ Adult mixes playdough, using either of the following recipes.

▶ When cool, place in a covered container or in a plastic bag.

▶ Child uses and reuses the playdough, molding it into shapes of her choice.

▶ Provide rolling pins for rolling the dough and bisquit cutters for making biscuits.

### Playdough Recipe #1:

| | |
|---|---|
| 1 tablespoon alum | 1 cup flour |
| 1 tablespoon cooking oil | 1/2 cup salt |
| 1 cup boiling water | |

Dissolve alum in oil and water. Mix flour and salt and add to water mixture. Knead when cool.

### Playdough Recipe #2:

| | |
|---|---|
| 1 cup flour | 1/2 cup salt |
| 1 cup water | 1 tablespoon vegetable oil |
| 2 teaspoons cream of tartar | |

Mix ingredients and heat until they form a ball. Knead after mixture cools. When cool, dough is ready for child's play.

**HOLIDAY ADAPTATIONS:** Add food coloring to water to make holiday colors: green and red for Christmas, red for Valentine's Day, pastels for Easter, or orange for Halloween.

**Bonus:** Great for muscle development!

# Home-made Finger Paint

**You Will Need:** Liquid starch, art paper, dry tempera.

## Activity:

▶ If commercial finger paint is not available, spread liquid starch on art paper and sprinkle dry tempera on the starch. As child works the starch and tempera together with finger(s), a finger paint consistency develops.

**You Will Need:** Finger paint ingredients (see recipe), burner, spoon, art paper.

## Activity:

▶ Adult prepares homemade finger paint using the following recipe:

**Homemade Finger Paint:**

    4 cups cold water
    6 teaspoons cornstarch
    tempera paint mix

Mix a small amount of cold water with cornstarch until smooth. Gradually add the remainder of the water. Adult cooks the mixture over low heat until it is clear and the consistency of pudding. Add tempera for color.

▶ When cool, spoon on art paper for child's finger painting fun.

**ADAPTATION:** Have child finger paint on a cookie sheet.

## Cups of Color

**You Will Need:** A muffin tin, water, food coloring (red, blue, green, and yellow), eyedroppers.

### Activity:

► Fill all the cups of a muffin tin with water.

► Drop red, blue, green, and yellow food coloring in each of four of the cups of water.

► Have child use eyedroppers to transfer colored water to other cups, thus creating different shades of color.

► By combining colors, child will create new colors: purple, chartreuse, brown, and so on.

**Bonus:** Great for small muscle development!

## Little Ships

**You Will Need:** Tongs or a meatball press, Styrofoam packaging chips, a bowl, a pan, water, a bathtub (optional).

### Activity:

► Have child use tongs or a meatball press to transfer Styrofoam chips from a bowl to a pan of water.

► If desired, fill a bathtub with water and allow child to use tongs to "float ships" in the tub.

**Bonus:** Great for muscle development and hand-eye coordination.

## Sock Sorting

**You Will Need:** Several pairs of child's socks, a box.

### Activity:

▶ Collect a number of pairs of old socks.

▶ Keep in a box for child's use.

▶ Have child match the socks and fold the tops over to make pairs.

**Bonus:** Great way to develop ability to see likeness and differences.

## Pantry Game

**You Will Need:** Labels from canned goods and food boxes, glue, poster board.

### Activity:

▶ Collect a duplicate set of labels from canned goods and food boxes—tuna fish, vegetable soup, shredded wheat, rice, and so on.

▶ Glue one set of labels on a poster board.

▶ Have child match the second set to the one on the poster board.

**Bonus:** This is the beginning of reading!

## Back Together

**You Will Need:** Scissors, magazines, glue, construction paper.

### Activity:

▶ Cut large magazine pictures into three or four vertical strips.

▶ Let child glue pictures back together on a background of construction paper.

**Bonus:** Great way to build whole/part relationship concepts!

## Button to Button

**You Will Need:** A large assortment of buttons, glue, an egg carton.

### Activity:

▶ Collect several different types of buttons: one-hole, two-hole, four-hole, red, white, black, blue, round, square, and so on.

▶ Glue one button on the inside of each section of an egg carton.

▶ Allow child to sort the remaining buttons into the sections according to an established criterion, such as number of holes, color, or shape.

**Bonus:** Good for seeing likenesses and differences.

## Number Bags

**You Will Need:** Large dried beans and enamel spray paint (or lima beans without spray paint), a marking pen, a sealable bag.

### Activity:

▶ Adult sprays large beans with enamel paint of desired colors; allow to dry. Spray the back of the beans. (This step is optional; if desired, use plain dried lima beans.)

▶ Write a number on the bottom of a sealable bag. Draw a vertical line down the middle of the bag.

▶ When paint is completely dry, place the desired number of beans into the bag and close it.

▶ Let child move the beans from one side to the other, leaving beans on either side of the line. Help child note that the total number of beans in the bag always remains the same. For example, if five beans are in the bag, child can manipulate the beans to see combinations that make five, such as four beans on one side of the vertical line and one bean on the other, etc.

**Bonus:** Great for understanding beginning math concepts.

## Card Matching

**You Will Need:** An old deck of cards, glue, a folder or poster board.

### Activity:

► Use an old deck of cards to create a matching game by taking one set of cards (2 through 10) and gluing them down in a folder or on a piece of poster board.

► Use the remainder of the deck as matching cards.

► Have child match other cards (2 through 10) to the set that has been glued down.

## Stacks and Stickers

**You Will Need:** Scissors, construction paper, self-adhesive sticker circles (eight to ten per child).

### Activity:

► Cut sheets of construction paper into large triangles.

► Cut the triangles into four horizontal pieces.

► Give child a set of the four pieces of paper and eight to ten self-adhesive sticker circles.

► Have child use the sticker circles to put the triangles back together.

**HOLIDAY ADAPTATION:** Use green construction paper and a variety of colored circles to make a decorated Christmas tree.

**Bonus:** Good way to develop whole/part relationship concepts!

## Bubble Machine

**You Will Need:** A straw, liquid detergent, water, a bowl, egg beater (optional).

### Activity:

▶ Teach child to blow air through a straw as opposed to sucking air into it.

▶ Make a solution of soapy water, using liquid detergent in a bowl.

▶ Give child a straw to make bubbles in the bowl by blowing through the straw.

**ADAPTATION:** Use egg beater instead of straw bubbles.

## Color Bottles

**You Will Need:** 1-liter plastic bottles with caps, water, food coloring (red and blue).

### Activity:

▶ Drop a few dots of red food coloring into 1-liter plastic bottles filled with water. Cap well.

▶ Let child roll the bottles back and forth and watch the color diffuse through the water.

▶ Uncap the bottles and add drops of blue. Re-cap. Repeat the rolling process to observe the creation of a new color, purple.

▶ Place bottles in the window for decoration.

**Bonus:** Concept development—diffusion!

## Soda
## Fizz

**You Will Need:** A teaspoon, baking soda, an empty 12-ounce soda bottle, vinegar, a balloon, a paper plate, two cups, a spoon, an eyedropper. Special adult supervision.

### Activity:

▶ Adult places a teaspoon of baking soda into an empty 12-ounce soda bottle and adds a teaspoon of vinegar. The two substances create a gas when mixed. To demonstrate this, adult places a balloon over the top of the soda bottle. It will expand from the gas. More of each substance will expand the balloon even more.

▶ Allow child to mix the two substances. Provide a paper plate, a small cup of vinegar, and a small cup of baking soda. Have child use a spoon to put the baking soda on the plate and an eyedropper to add the vinegar. The mixture will fizz.

## Playdough

**You Will Need:** Different colors of playdough (see page 16 for recipes).

### Activity:

▶ Using playdough recipe, adult makes two different batches of playdough—one colored red and one colored yellow.

▶ Give child two playdough balls, one of each color. As child mixes the two colors, they will discover the creation of orange.

▶ Continue with other colors.

**HOLIDAY ADAPTATION:** Make pumpkins for Halloween.

**Bonus:** Concept development—mixing two colors creates a third color.

## Color Tubes

**You Will Need:** A piece of clear plastic tubing (at least 1/2 inch in diameter and 30 inches long), two corks (to fit the tubing), food coloring (two colors).

## Activity:

► Adult prepares color tube by using a piece of clear plastic tubing at least 1/2 inch in diameter and 30 inches long.

► Put a cork in one end and fill with water. Add a few drops of food coloring and cork the other end.

► Remove the cork from the opposite end and add a different color. Replace the cork.

► Child wiggles the tube or turns it end over end; the color from each end will work to the center and mix.

**Bonus:** Concept development—color mixing!

# THREE

# Things to Think About

## Inch by Inch

**You Will Need:** Scissors, magazines, manila folders.

### Activity:

► Cut a variety of interesting pictures from magazines.

► Place each picture inside a manila folder.

► Pull each picture out of its folder, revealing parts of the picture a little at a time.

► Let child guess what the picture is.

► When guessing is over, reveal the whole picture and discuss.

**ADAPTATION:** Cut small windows in the outside (cover) of the folder.

**Bonus:** Encourages the understanding of whole/part relationships.

## Alliteration

### Activity:

► Give child several examples of sentences with alliteration, such as "Harry Hippo hops high," or "Barney Bear bounces balls."

► Then child creates her own sentences with words beginning with the same sound.

**Bonus:** Good for language development!

## Silly Sentences

**37**

### Activity:

▶ Create a series of silly sentences for child to repeat that have words that rhyme.

**EXAMPLES:** "I know a lady with knobby knees
Who's always eating Cheddar cheese."

"I like ice cream in my soup,
By myself, or in a group."

▶ Allow child to make up silly sentences with rhyming words.

**Bonus:** Good activity for the car!

## How Many?

**38**

**You Will Need:** A tub, water, measuring utensils (cups, spoons, and so on), larger containers (funnels, clear plastic liter bottles, and so on).

### Activity:

▶ Provide a tub of water and several measuring utensils, such as measuring cups and measuring spoons. Also provide larger containers, such as funnels and clear plastic liter bottles.

▶ Let child experiment to see how many cups of water it takes to fill a larger container or how many tablespoons of water to fill a cup.

**Bonus:** Good way to establish measurement concepts.

## Candy Counting

**You Will Need:** A bag, multicolored candies or different-shaped crackers.

### Activity:

▶ Give child a bag of multicolored candies.

▶ Have her separate the candies into sets by color.

▶ Extend this activity by asking child to count the candies in each set. For example, ask how many yellow ones she has, how many green ones she has, and how many red ones she has.

**ADAPTATION:** Give child a handful of different-shaped crackers. Ask child to separate the crackers into sets by shape. Have her count the number of crackers in each set.

## What Is Half?

**You Will Need:** A knife, two apples, scissors, two pieces of paper, two glasses, water.

### Activity:

▶ Tell the child that dividing something in half means dividing it fairly between two people.

▶ Adult illustrates this concept by cutting apples in half, cutting paper in half, and pouring a full glass of water partially into a second glass so that each glass is half full.

▶ As each item is divided, ask the child which part she would want. The child should notice that it wouldn't matter.

▶ Cut a piece of paper and an apple into unequal portions and ask the same question.

**Bonus:** Great for building a foundation for fractions!

## Will This Dissolve?

**You Will Need:** Five clear glasses, water, a rock, salt, a leaf, sugar, pepper.

### Activity:

▶ Fill glasses with water.

▶ Show child the following items: a rock, salt, a leaf, sugar, and pepper.

▶ Ask child to predict whether or not the items will dissolve in water.

▶ Test each item with the child.

▶ Verify predictions.

**Bonus:** Great for critical thinking.

## Ping-Pong Volley

**You Will Need:** Masking tape, a Ping-Pong ball, a book, a straw, a paper towel tube.

### Activity:

▶ Place two long strips of masking tape 5 feet apart on the floor.

▶ Ask child how he could move a Ping-Pong ball from one taped line to the other without touching it. Possibilities include blowing with the mouth, fanning with a book, blowing with a straw, blowing through a paper towel tube, and so on.

▶ Let child try suggestions.

▶ Observe which method accomplishes the task the fastest.

▶ Child and adult position themselves on opposite lines and move the ball back and forth.

**Bonus:** Good for problem solving!

## Is This Cup Full?

**You Will Need:** A glass, pebbles, salt or sand, water.

## Activity:

▶ Fill a glass with pebbles. Ask child if the glass if full. If she doesn't think so, have her add pebbles until she agrees that the glass is full. Then ask if she thinks anything else will fit into the glass. She will probably say "no."

▶ Pour either salt or sand into the same glass. The child will be surprised to see the glass holds more. Call attention to how the salt or sand fills in the spaces left between the pebbles. Now ask again if the glass is full. The child will probably say "yes."

▶ Pour water into the same glass. The child will again be surprised. Ask why the glass could hold the water.

▶ Ask child if the process could work in reverse, starting with a full glass of water and adding salt and rocks. Try suggestions.

**Bonus:** Great for critical thinking!

## Separate Solids

**You Will Need:** A cup of beans, a cup of salt, a cup of rice, four large bowls, a strainer, a colander.

### Activity:

► Mix beans, salt, and rice together in a bowl.

► Provide child with a strainer and a colander and tell him to separate the items in the bowl into three separate bowls: one with beans, one with salt, and one with rice.

► After the child is successful, ask him if he can think of another way to accomplish the task.

**Bonus:** Good for problem solving!

## Can Race

**You Will Need:** Two coffee cans, several small items (a block, a crayon, a roll of tape, a small book, and so on), masking tape.

### Activity:

► Give child two coffee cans and several smaller items that can be placed into the cans.

► Let child explore the way different items placed inside the cans affect the cans' ability to roll.

► Use masking tape to mark a finish line and have child race the cans.

**Bonus:** Good for critical thinking!

## Sacks of Air

**You Will Need:** One lunch-sized paper sack.

### Activity:

▶ Give child lunch-sized paper sack to blow up.

▶ Have child feel the sack and observe fullness.

▶ After several blowups, let the child pop the sack to let the air escape.

▶ Ask child if he can think of another way to let the air escape.

**Bonus:** Concept development—air fills space!

## Air Pushers

**You Will Need:** Small, light items (paper, feathers, Styrofoam packaging chips, and so on); masking tape; empty plastic catsup, mustard, or detergent dispensers.

### Activity:

▶ Place small items in a circle of masking tape on the floor.

▶ Let child try to "squirt" (push with air) the items out of the circle with empty plastic dispensers.

**Bonus:** Concept development—air moves things!

## Raisin Elevator

**You Will Need:** Clear carbonated soda water, a clear glass, four or five raisins.

### Activity:

▶ Pour soda water into a clear glass.

▶ Drop four or five raisins into the glass.

▶ After 40 to 60 seconds, child will observe raisins moving up and down in the glass.

▶ Help child draw the conclusion that the air bubbles cause the upward movement.

▶ Let child observe the glass later in the day when the carbonation has ceased. This will reinforce the role of the air bubbles in lifting the raisins.

## Invisible Names

**You Will Need:** Cooking oil, butcher paper, a light source, a damp sponge.

### Activity:

▶ Have child use finger to write names or draw pictures on butcher paper with cooking oil.

▶ Have child hold paper up to a light source. Names or pictures will become visible.

▶ Child can try to wipe the writing off with a damp sponge, but it will not go away.

**Bonus:** Concept development—oil and water don't mix.

## Wave Maker

**You Will Need:** One clear plastic bottle (at least 10 inches high) with a top, denatured alcohol, blue food coloring, cooking oil, glue.

### Activity:

▶ Adult fills a clear plastic bottle three-fourths full with denatured alcohol.

▶ Adult adds blue food coloring to make the alcohol deep blue. Fill the bottle with cooking oil, leaving a small distance at the top. Glue the top on for safety.

▶ The substances will not mix and the water will spread like a wave over the oil when moved up and down.

▶ Place the bottle on the table for child's use, observation, and questions.

**Bonus:** Concept development—oil and water don't mix!

## Ice in a Bag

**You Will Need:** Ice cubes, one sealable bag, a freezer.

### Activity:

▶ Let child put ice cubes in a bag. Seal the bags.

▶ Discuss how the ice feels hard and cold.

▶ Place the bag on a table until the cubes have melted. Talk about the change that has taken place, using the terms *solid* and *liquid*.

▶ Ask child how to return the liquid to a solid. Test. Return bag to freezer.

**Bonus:** Concept development—change of state!

## Jiggling Gelatin

**You Will Need:** Unmade flavored gelatin, boiling water, a bowl, a spoon.

### Activity:

▶ Adult makes gelatin according to package instructions. Call attention to the solid state of the gelatin in the package. Have child note the change to a liquid when the gelatin is dissolved in water.

▶ Later, serve the gelatin as a snack, noting the change back to a solid.

**ADAPTATION:** Use less water than the recipe requires. Cut the gelatin into cubes and serve as finger food.

**HOLIDAY ADAPTATIONS:** Make red gelatin for Valentine's Day, green and red for Christmas, or orange for Halloween.

**Bonus:** Concept development—changes of state.

## Wood Sanding

**You Will Need:** One block of wood, a writing utensil, one piece of sandpaper.

### Activity:

▶ Give child a block of wood with her name written on it and a piece of sandpaper. After the child has rubbed sandpaper on the wood, question her: "How does it feel?" It should feel warm and smooth.

▶ Child will also discover that sandpapering erodes, or wears away, the surface when she sees the name disappear.

**Bonus:** Concept development—erosion!

## Trotting Horses

**You Will Need:** A long table.

### Activity:

► Ask child if he has ever seen a cowboy movie in which someone puts an ear to the ground to find out if horses are coming.

► Explain that sound carries through the ground and through other materials, such as tabletops. The sound also sounds louder this way.

► Adult and child sit at opposite ends of a long table and take turns scratching the underside of the table. Have child put an ear on the table while the adult scratches under the table. The listening child will note how much louder the scratching sound is.

## Sand Creation

**You Will Need:** Two rocks, dark paper, a magnifying glass.

### Activity:

► Give child two rocks to rub together over a piece of dark paper.

► Child will see the sand that is produced by the rubbing action.

► Have child use a magnifying glass to see the rock shape of the sand.

**Bonus:** Concept development—erosion!

## Filter Game

**You Will Need:** A plastic tub, water, materials for filtering and straining (Styrofoam packaging chips, gravel of varying sizes, leaves, a plastic colander, a tea strainer, a funnel, and so on).

### Activity:

► Fill a plastic tub with water. Provide a variety of materials for child to discover how to filter or strain objects from water.

## Kitchen Tools

**You Will Need:** A manual eggbeater, a potato masher, soapy water, a banana.

### Activity:

► Collect items from the kitchen, such as a manual eggbeater and a potato masher.

► Set up opportunities for child to use these items to make work easy. For example, use an eggbeater and soapy water to make bubbles or a potato masher to mash a banana.

► Have child think of and experiment with other appropriate tools from the kitchen.

**Bonus:** Concept development—tools make work easier.

FOUR

# Things for Pretending

## Sheet Tents

**You Will Need:** A bed sheet or large piece of fabric; a fence; clothespins; a picnic table, heavy objects, or string.

### Activity:

▶ On hot, sunny days, adult can create shade by making sheet tents.

▶ Clip a bed sheet (or other large piece of fabric) to a fence with clothespins.

▶ Secure the opposite end of the sheet by placing it under picnic table legs or by placing heavy objects (such as tires) on the edges of the sheet.

▶ An alternate method is to clip the sheet to the fence and tie the opposite corners of the sheet to a tree or a piece of play equipment.

▶ "Build" several tents to encourage dramatic play.

## Giants and Elves

**You Will Need:** A drum (or empty coffee can with plastic lid.

### Activity:

▶ Using a drum, beat loudly and softly while child walks around the room.

▶ Have child tiptoe like an elf to soft music and walk like a giant to loud music.

## Bath Time for Baby

**You Will Need:** A table, towels, a baby tub, water, washable dolls, washcloths, mild soap, doll clothes.

### Activity:

► Cover a table with towels.

► Place a baby tub partially filled with water on the table.

► Provide washable dolls, extra towels, washcloths, and mild soap.

► Let child bathe "babies" and redress them.

**ADAPTATION:** Use the kitchen sink if a baby tub is not available.

**Bonus:** Good activity for adapting to a new baby in the home.

## Boat Talk

**You Will Need:** Masking tape.

### Activity:

► Tape a boat shape on the floor.

► Let child stand in the "boat" and describe what he would do if he were in a real boat.

**ADAPTATION:** Tape a rectangle to serve as a stage. Have child describe what he would do on the stage.

## Dancing Shadows

**You Will Need:** Adhesive tape and a sheet (or a movie screen), a high-intensity lamp or projector light, a record or musical tape and a player.

### Activity:

► Tape a sheet on the wall or set up a movie screen.

► Adult creates a light source by using a high-intensity lamp or projector light.

► While playing music, let child create the movements of a particular animal (bird, kangaroo, lion, and so on) while dancing in front of the light source and making shadows on the wall.

## Box House

**You Will Need:** A large appliance box, scissors, tape, 1- to 2-foot-square pieces of cloth, child's scissors, construction paper, glue, tempera paint (optional).

### Activity:

► Obtain a large appliance box to use as a playhouse.

► Adult cuts doors and windows in it.

► Tape cloth curtains on the windows.

► Have child cut flowers from construction paper to glue on the outside.

► Child may also choose to paint the outside of the house using tempera paint.

► Child will create other decorating opportunities as she plays with the house.

## Butterfly Wings

**You Will Need:** Adhesive tape, streamers (eight or ten 10 to 15 inches long), computer paper or newspaper, a record or musical tape and a player.

### Activity:

▶ Tape four or five 10- to 15-inch streamers on left edges of two pieces of computer paper or newspaper.

▶ Roll from right end to make two long cuffs for child's lower arms and tape, being sure that the streamers flow freely.

▶ Play music and have child move around the room, fluttering "wings."

## Paper Clip Fish

**You Will Need:** A magnet, a small fishing pole (or newspaper and a piece of string 2 to 3 feet long), construction paper, scissors, paper clips, a small plastic wading pool or masking tape.

### Activity:

▶ Tie a magnet on the string of a small fishing pole (or a homemade fishing pole of rolled-up newspaper with a string attached).

▶ Place a paper clip on a cut-out construction paper fish.

▶ Place the fish in a small plastic wading pool or a "pond" taped on the floor with masking tape. Let child "fish," attracting the paper clip with the magnet.

**ADAPTATION:** Tape a boat shape on the floor and place fish outside the boat on the floor. Let child fish out of the boat.

**Bonus:** Concept development—magnets attract metal objects.

## Mega-phones

**You Will Need:** Large pieces of heavy paper, writing utensils, child's scissors, a stapler or adhesive tape.

### Activity:

▶ Prepare a megaphone pattern as shown in the illustration. (Enlarge pattern on page 48.)

▶ Using heavy paper, let child trace around the pattern and cut out if appropriate.

▶ When megaphones are rolled and taped or stapled together, the child can go outside and practice "cheerleading."

▶ Caution child against holding a megaphone close to anyone's ear.

## Shoe Skating

**You Will Need:** A waltz record or waltz tape and a player, different floor surfaces (carpet, tile, and so on).

### Activity:

▶ Put on waltz music and tell child to "pretend-skate" across the floor.

▶ Have child skate across a different type of floor surface. Compare the different surfaces.

▶ Play another song and let the child skate with shoes off. Compare socks and bare feet, if appropriate.

**Bonus:** Concept development—friction!

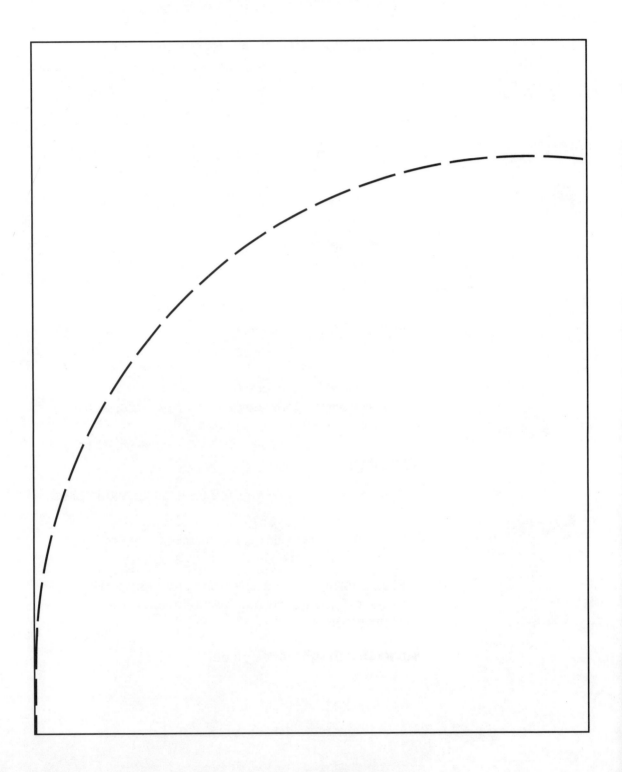

# FIVE

# Things for "Moving and Grooving"

## Groovy Moves

### Activity:

► Have child demonstrate ways to move other than on his feet. For example, he might crawl on his hands and knees, scoot on his seat, roll or wiggle like a worm, and so on.

► Have child demonstrate how he would look in a strong wind, on a hot day, in a snow storm, or in a flood.

► Adult guesses what type of day the person moving is imagining.

## Scarf Dancing

**You Will Need:** One scarf, long piece of light-weight cloth, or crepe paper streamer; a record or musical tape and a player.

### Activity:

► Provide child with a scarf, a long piece of light-weight cloth, or a crepe paper streamer.

► Play music.

► Have child wave "scarves" and move to the rhythm of the music.

## Grass Skirts

**You Will Need:** Scissors, whole sheets of newspaper, masking tape, a record or musical tape and a player.

### Activity:

▶ Make a "grass skirt" by cutting whole sheets of newspaper in strips, leaving a waistband at the top of each.

▶ Tape the skirt together at the child's waist with masking tape.

▶ Allow child to respond freely to music.

## Olympic Streamers

**You Will Need:** Newspaper, adhesive tape, crepe paper, a record or musical tape and a player.

### Activity:

▶ Roll up newspapers into 6-inch wands; tape together to hold.

▶ Tape a long, thin strip of crepe paper to each wand.

▶ Play music and have child make circles and other figures with streamers and move rhythmically around the room.

**Bonus:** Great exercise!

## Musical Bean- bags

**You Will Need:** One beanbag, a record or musical tape and a player.

### Activity:

► Give child a beanbag.

► Play music. Have child move around with beanbag on his head, on either shoulder, or on either elbow.

► When the music stops, have child "freeze," holding the position he is in until the music resumes.

**Bonus:** Great birthday party group game!

## Bottle Maracas

**You Will Need:** Rice or gravel, clear plastic shampoo or detergent bottles with lids, glue.

### Activity:

► Make maracas by placing rice or gravel in empty, clear plastic shampoo or detergent bottles.

► Glue the lids on for safety.

► Let child use the maracas as instruments.

## Drums and Sticks

**You Will Need:** Gallon cans with plastic lids, pencils with erasers or sticks with cloth balls tied to their ends, 10- to 12-inch-long dowel sticks or wooden kitchen spoons.

### Activity:

▶ Use empty gallon cans with plastic lids for simple drums. Have child tap the drums with the eraser end of pencils or with sticks that have balls of cloth tied on their ends.

▶ Cut dowel sticks into 10- to 12-inch lengths to make rhythm sticks, or use wooden kitchen spoons for rhythm sticks.

▶ Have child play the sticks by tapping them on the floor or by tapping them together.

## Pom-Poms

**You Will Need:** Newspaper, adhesive tape, scissors, a record or musical tape and a player.

### Activity:

▶ Prepare pom-poms by rolling half sheets of newspaper into stick shapes. Tape the bottom half to form a handle and cut the top half into strips.

▶ Play music with varying rhythms, from marches to hulas.

▶ Have child "swish" pom-poms as she moves to the rhythm of the music.

**HOLIDAY ADAPTATION:** Have a Fourth of July parade using march music.

**Bonus:** Great for exercise!

**SIX**

# Things for Under-standing My Family and "Me"

## Sally Sad and Harriet Happy

**You Will Need:** <u>Two paper plates,</u> two sticks (about 12 inches long each), marking pens or other art supplies for making faces.

### Activity:

▶ Prepare two paper plate faces on sticks, one with a happy face and one with a sad face.

▶ Child holds plate faces and explains reasons for Sally being sad and Harriet being happy.

**EXAMPLES:**  "I'm Sally Sad, and I'm sad because . . ."

"I'm Harriet Happy, and I'm happy because . . ."

## Freckle Names

**You Will Need:** A writing utensil, construction paper, glue, a hole punch, newspaper.

### Activity:

▶ Write child's name on construction paper.

▶ Have child outline her name with glue on construction paper.

▶ Give child a handful of construction paper hole punches and have her sprinkle these over the paper. Shake off the excess onto a newspaper.

**Bonus:** Great for name recognition.

## Chore Checkoff

**You Will Need:** A straight edge, construction paper, a writing utensil.

### Activity:

► Provide child with a ruled construction paper chart for chores—making the bed, carrying dishes to the sink, and so on.

► Have child mark the squares in left to right order for each day he completes the chores.

**Bonus:** This helps children internalize left-to-right progression.

## Broken Names

**You Will Need:** A writing utensil, one large card, scissors.

### Activity:

► Write child's name on a large card.

► Cut the card into puzzle pieces, making each letter a puzzle piece.

► Make the name card self-correcting by cutting between letters in different ways.

► Have child put letters back together to spell name correctly.

**Bonus:** Great for name recognition and understanding of whole/part relationship.

Write David's
Name on a
Card for
his table
give him some
special pens

## Tree of Hands

*Mommy's Hands Like to*
*Handprints*
*Nice Paper*

**You Will Need:** Writing utensils, green paper, scissors.

### Activity:

▶ Let child trace around hands of family members, including uncles, aunts, and cousins, on green paper.

▶ Cut out the hands.

▶ Write names on the paper hands to identify.

▶ Arrange on the wall in the shape of a tree, starting with the bottom row and overlapping successive rows like house shingles.

**HOLIDAY ADAPTATION:** Place a star on top and paint tips of fingers red to make a decorated Christmas tree.

## Baby Up

**You Will Need:** Pictures of child at various ages.

### Activity:

▶ Have child find pictures of herself as a baby, as a toddler, and at present age.

▶ Discuss what a child can and cannot do at each age.

▶ Sequence pictures chronologically on a chart.

**ADAPTATION:** Use magazine pictures if necessary.

## 82

## Family Tree

**You Will Need:** Pictures of child's family members.

### Activity:

▶ Help child collect pictures of grandparents, parents, and themselves.

▶ Place family groupings in chronological order as child talks about lineage.

**ADAPTATION:** Use magazine pictures if necessary to categorize age groups.

Use
Jills
Frame

# SEVEN

# Things to Make a Better World

## Pinecone Bird Feeders

**You Will Need:** Waxed paper, a spreading knife, smooth peanut butter, pinecones, bird seed, string.

### Activity:

► Place waxed paper on the table.

► Spread a thin layer of smooth peanut butter on the waxed paper.

► Have child roll a pinecone in the peanut butter and then in bird seed.

► Attach a string to the pinecone and hang it on a tree.

**HOLIDAY ADAPTATION:** Hang a number of pinecones in a small tree with Christmas ribbon to prepare a Christmas tree for birds.

**Bonus:** Great for environmental awareness!

## Litter Brigade

**You Will Need:** One empty cereal box, cord.

### Activity:

► Use a cereal box and a piece of cord to make a litter collector for the child to hang over her shoulder.

► Go for a walk together, with child carrying a litter collector to fill with items that have been thrown on the ground.

**Bonus:** Good for environmental awareness!

## 85

## Trash Truck

**You Will Need:** A hole punch, a medium-sized box, a small rope (about a yard long), marker.

### Activity:

▶ To help develop experience in sharing responsibilities for group living, adult prepares a trash truck by punching holes in a box and inserting a small rope tied as a handle.

▶ Using marker, make a sign on the side of the box: *Trash Truck.*

▶ With adult, child can pull the Trash Truck around the neighborhood or a park and place trash in the "truck." The "driver" should empty the trash into a can.

**ADAPTATION:** Use the Trash Truck to collect garbage after a picnic.

**Bonus:** Good for environmental awareness!

## 86

## Can Collection

**You Will Need:** A large box.

### Activity:

▶ Start a collection of empty aluminum cans in a large box.

▶ With the child, take the cans to a recycling center each week. Save the receipts.

▶ At the end of a given time, have the child help select an item to buy with the proceeds.

**ADAPTATION:** Have child select an inexpensive item for future purchase and see how many cans must be collected to purchase item.

**Bonus:** Great for environmental awareness!

# EIGHT

# Things to do Outdoors

## Wet Sand

**You Will Need:** A watering can, sandbox, sticks, combs, potato mashers.

### Activity:

► Water the sand in a sandbox.

► Child kneels at the perimeter of the sandbox, leaning into the sandbox and making designs in the sand with sticks, combs, and potato mashers.

► Provide a watering can for remoistening the sand when needed.

**ADAPTATION:** Place moist sand in a cake pan.

## Liquid Movers

**You Will Need:** A tub, water, objects that pick up water (a baster, eyedroppers, and so on), an 8-ounce cup, writing utensils, paper.

### Activity:

► Give child a tub of water and a variety of objects that pick up water, such as basters, syringes, and eyedroppers.

► Let child experiment with each item. Have her use tally marks to record how many times each item must be used to fill up an 8-ounce cup.

**Bonus:** Good for muscle development and coordination.

## Mud Cakes

**You Will Need:** A sandbox, small buckets, water, sticks or candles.

### Activity:

▶ On a warm, sunny day, plan an outdoor activity in the sandbox.

▶ Provide small buckets of water to make mud cakes. Provide sticks (or real candles) to use as birthday candles.

▶ When child has made a mud cake, ask him to place three candles on his cake.

▶ Ask child to add one more candle. Ask, "Now how many do you have?"

▶ Continue the process at the appropriate level of understanding.

**Bonus:** Great for building addition concepts.

## Tom Sawyer Painting

**You Will Need:** Small plastic buckets, water, housepainters' brushes.

### Activity:

▶ Give the child a small plastic bucket of water and housepainters' brushes.

▶ Let her "paint" the sidewalk, the side of the house, and wheeled toys. Child will enjoy the painting and she will discover that the water "goes away."

**Bonus:** Concept development—evaporation!

## Wind Wheels

**You Will Need:** Scissors; one plastic lid; strips of newspaper, crepe paper, ribbon, or cloth.

### Activity:

► Adult cuts a large circle out of a plastic lid so that only a rim remains.

► Have child tape strips of newspaper, crepe paper, ribbon, or cloth onto one side of the rim.

► Outside, let child clutch the rim and run to make the streamers "fly."

## Water Moving

**You Will Need:** Two plastic tubs, water, materials for moving water (plastic bottles and jars in a variety of sizes, plastic measuring spoons, turkey basters, plastic straws, eyedroppers, funnels, and so on).

### Activity:

► Fill one plastic tub with water. Provide a variety of materials for child to learn how to move water from the full tub to the empty one: plastic bottles and jars, plastic measuring spoons, turkey basters, plastic straws, eyedroppers, funnels, and so on.

► Provide both short, wide plastic jars and tall, thin plastic bottles.

**Bonus:** Concept development—tools make work easier.

## Tire Garden

**You Will Need:** A tire or tires, garden soil, flower seeds or carrot and onion seeds.

### Activity:

▶ Make a tire garden by filling a tire or tires with garden soil.

▶ Let child plant flower seeds.

▶ Over time, have child pull weeds and water.

▶ Enjoy the flowers when they bloom.

**ADAPTATION:** Plant carrots and onions in a tire garden, following directions on the seed packages. Have child water and weed the garden. When the vegetables are mature, pull up for child to see and feel. Cook, if appropriate, and eat.

**Bonus:** Concept development—plants and vegetables grow from seeds.

## Leaf Bracelets

**You Will Need:** Masking tape, an outdoor area with several varieties of trees.

### Activity:

▶ Wrap a piece of masking tape (sticky side out) around child's wrist and adult's wrist.

▶ Go on a nature walk and collect one leaf from each of several trees.

▶ Stick the leaves to the bracelets (masking tape) and create a great accessory!

**ADAPTATION:** Make belts, head bands, or other accessory items.

## 95

## Treasure Hunt

**You Will Need:** One sack, an outdoor area with several varieties of trees, a large box, several shoe boxes, adhesive tape.

### Activity:

► After giving child a sack for collecting, go on a leaf treasure hunt in the backyard or in a park. Assist child in noting that trees can be identified by their distinctive leaves.

► Place collected leaves in a large box on a table. Arrange shoe boxes on the table with a different leaf taped to each box lid. Place lids upright at the end of shoe boxes.

► Let child choose a leaf from the large box, then match it with a leaf on one of the shoe box lids and place it in that shoe box.

**Bonus:** Great for seeing likenesses and differences!

## 96

## Looking Loops

Out in a meadow

**You Will Need:** Several pieces of cord or heavy string (at least a yard long each), a magnifying glass.

### Activity:

► Using pieces of cord or heavy string, make several loops by tying ends to make circles.

► Place loops at various locations around the yard (away from ants).

► Let child look inside the circles and see how many insects can be seen.

► Give child a magnifying glass to help observation.

► Extend activity to look for rocks and plants, too.

## Ant Watching

**You Will Need:** Chicken bones, special adult supervision.

### Activity:

▶ After a picnic, leave chicken bones on the picnic table to attract ants. Watch from a distance.

▶ Child will be fascinated with the speed that ants arrive and start working to clean the bones.

▶ When ants are gone, remove bones to avoid harm to dogs or cats.

## Ant Helpers

**You Will Need:** Freshly collected seashells, a can.

### Activity:

▶ To remove the odor from freshly collected seashells, bury shells in a can in the ground. Ants will clean off any remaining meat.

▶ After a few days, dig up the can. The shells will be clean.

▶ Let child wash the shells and place them on a table for display.

## Bug
## Bottles

**You Will Need:** A clean empty bleach bottle, scissors, a nylon stocking.

### Activity:

▶ To observe live insects, make a bug bottle from a clean bleach bottle.

▶ Adult cuts out large circles in the sides of bottle so the insects can be observed.

▶ Place the cut-out bottle in a stocking. Put insects inside and tie at the top.

▶ Release the insects at the end of the day so child will learn respect for freedom and life.

## Sandbox
## Tools

**You Will Need:** Clean, empty bleach bottles with lids, scissors.

### Activity:

▶ Adult uses clean bleach bottles to make buckets, sand scoops, and funnels for child's play.

▶ To make buckets, cut the bottles in half and use the bottoms.

▶ To make scoops, use the top halves with handles. Screw on the caps.

▶ To make funnels, remove the caps from the top halves of the bottles.

**Bonus:** Concept development—recycling!

# Notes

**Notes**

**Notes**

**Notes**

## More great books for parents and kids:

### SCHOOL'S OUT *by Joan Bergstrom*

"The book for parents who would like the children's out-of-school time to be spent developing initiative, responsibility, and creativity—as well as having fun."
> —Dr. Benjamin Spock

The best-ever resource book for after school, weekends, and vacations. Packed full of ideas for activities and projects, it also includes hints on making chores more fun, and on safety for latchkey children.
$13.95 paper, 330 pages

### ALL THE BEST CONTESTS FOR KIDS *by Joan Bergstrom & Craig Bergstrom*

Hundreds of contests for kids to enter, in fields from art to computers to sewing to roller skating. Complete entry information for every contest, plus hints for starting your own contest, or getting your writing and artwork published. Winner of a 1990 Parent's Choice Award.
$9.95 paper, 288 pages

### YOU ARE YOUR CHILD'S FIRST TEACHER *by Rahima Baldwin*

"Here is an extraordinary work for those who want to develop a truly intelligent child and, in the process, unlock new levels of their own intelligence and spirit."
> —Joseph Chilton Pearce

A new look at what parents can do with and for their children from the very first moment through school age to enhance their development in a caring, supportive way.
$12.95 paper or $19.95 cloth, 380 pages

### NIGHTMARE HELP *by Ann Sayre Wiseman*

Simple, effective, hands-on techniques that really help. Shows how adults can use children's natural love of drawing in working out frightening and confusing dreams.
$9.95 paper, 96 pages

### GRANDMA AND GRANDPA ARE SPECIAL PEOPLE *by Barbara Polland, Ph.D.*

"For every adult and child who had a grandma or grandpa who tweaked their nose, baked raisin cookies, or toddled them on their knee, and for all those others who wished they had."
> —Virginia Satir, family therapist & author

A book about getting to know grandparents—what they are, who they are, and the special roles they can play in our lives. Illustrated.
$7.95 paper, 80 pages

### THE GLIDING FLIGHT *by John Collins*

Twenty wonderfully inventive origami paper airplanes, made entirely by folding—no glue or cutting required. Clear step-by-step instructions, illustrated with photos and line drawings. The author is the winner of an international paper airplane contest.
$7.95 paper, 160 pages

**LOVING THE EARTH** *by Fredric Lehrman*

A children's primer on the planet Earth. Beautiful photographs and paintings show the many faces of our planet, and make a plea for loving and protecting it. Shows specific, simple things that we can all do to help.
$17.95 clothbound, 48 pages

**CATSWALK** *written and illustrated by Trina Robbins*

The magical fantasy tale of Girl, who was raised by the last of the talking cats. Following the map left by a mysterious stranger, the two set off on a Catswalk—a journey of adventure and self-discovery. Full-color illustrations.
$17.95 cloth, 64 pages

**A GIFT FOR MISS MILO** *by Jan Wahl, illustrated by Jeff Grove*

"A book for all ages. Mattie and Miss Milo are a lovely pair of heroines and Mattie's telling of the story as she does her own growing is a delight."
    —Madeleine L'Engle, author of *A Wrinkle in Time*

"With haunting prose and an aura of old-fashioned mystery, Wahl…spins this captivating tale of love and betrayal, of reality and illusion…splendid paintings."
    —*Publisher's Weekly*

A beautifully illustrated and haunting intergenerational tale of love and longing.
$13.95 cloth, 96 pages

**THE PUMPKIN BLANKET** *by Deborah Turney Zagwyn*

In this picture book, the pumpkin crop is endangered just before Halloween, and five-year-old Clee must give up her beloved blanket to save it. But she gains a wonderful holiday, and learns the value of sharing.
$14.95 cloth, 32 pages

**ANIMALIA** *by Barbara Berger*

Thirteen short animal tales from around the world, each hand-lettered and complete on two lavishly illuminated color pages.
$12.95 paper, 64 pages

Available from your local bookstore, or order direct from the publisher. Please include $1.25 shipping & handling for the first book, and 50 cents for each additional book. California residents include local sales tax. Write for our free complete catalog of over 400 books and tapes.

Ship to:

Name _____

Address _____

City _____ State _____ Zip _____

Phone _____

TEN SPEED PRESS   P.O. Box 7123   Berkeley, CA 94707
For VISA or Mastercard orders call (510) 845-8414

We also carry a line of full-color glow-in-the-dark posters of dinosaurs, rainforest life, space stations, and other subjects kids love. Call or write for details.